Enjoy

Best

Val Portelle

AKA Poinks

About the Author

If you ever meet the author, be careful what you say. Any chance remark could become the subject of her next book. Voinks is a prolific writer who loves people, life and never suffers writer's block. Her main problem is finding time to put pen to paper and keeping up with her friends when inspiration takes over. You have been warned.

Dedicated to my Mother Lily R.I.P

To Delphine. I 'invented' the name to suit the story, just as I met a lady of that name who has since become a good friend.

Voinks

ABC-Destiny

A CIP catalogue record for this title is available from the British Library.

ISBN 978 1 78455 696 9 (Paperback)
ISBN 978 1 78455 698 3 (Hardback)

www.austinmacauley.com

First Published (2015)
Austin Macauley Publishers Ltd.
25 Canada Square
Canary Wharf
London
E14 5LB

Printed and bound in Great Britain

Contents

ABC-Destiny

Chapter 1:

Abigail

Hi. My name is Abigail. Yuck, not surprising then that I'm normally known to my friends as Ay.

I was brought up in a white, middle-class suburban background with a mother and a father and an elder brother. Almost the regulation two point five children as Mum lost one baby after my brother was born, which was why they adopted me when she found out she couldn't have any more.

So I was theoretically the youngest.

Dad worked for the local council earning a normal middle-class wage, and we lived in a three bedroom house in the suburbs of London.

I went to the local junior school, passed my eleven-plus and progressed to grammar school.

University was not the normal next step, but I did have a good education which enabled me to get a job at sixteen with decent career prospects.

Those were not the days of political correctness or equality of the genders. There was still disparity between male and female wages, but I managed to rise through the ranks to become a fairly senior manager.

It was not easy, but I had been brought up to understand that you got nothing unless you worked for it.

A lot of my peers left school without any qualifications and ended up working for peanuts in the local take-away.

So maybe the times I stayed in studying while they were out clubbing and meeting boys was worth it in the long run.

Although not rich we paid our bills on time, had a good second-hand car and enjoyed a holiday once a year.

The mortgage payments on the house were kept up to date, and by the time my parents retired it would be paid off. They would have their pensions to start to enjoy the life for which they had worked so hard.

Even if life was sometimes a struggle we had pride in that whatever we had was bought and paid for. We could look at our possessions and enjoy the fact that they were earned honestly by hard graft.

Chapter 2:

Beatrice

I'm called Bea.

Don't know why you want to know about me. Everything in my life is crap.

Yeah, life's a bitch.

My mum brung me up as a single parent. Was gonna say the taboo F word but don't know if that would be allowed.

No idea who my father was, but I've had plenty of so-called uncles for as long as I can remember. Think Mum is trying to regain her lost youth and goes for anything in trousers what makes her feel good.

Some of them were OK, but most treated me as a nuisance getting in the way of their sex life, which was the only thing they were interested in. The rest looked on me as fair game despite my age.

I grew up quick and learnt to defend myself from groping hands by a quick kick in the B…, which was the only language they understood.

When I tried to tell Mum she thought it was just jealousy or teenage hormones, so at the end of the day I was on my own.

If you want to know anything about how to get through the social form filling or how to get a pay-out from the system, ask me. I'm an expert.

If things get hairy, all you have to do is move to a different address and by the time they've caught up with your past record you've moved on again.

Playing the game. You have to take advantage when you can – just to make life worth living.

If you want something special and haven't got the cash, well the shops are full. If you get caught you just go into the 'poor little me' routine and most of the time the courts accept it.

As I said life's a bitch, but you learn to fight it, however and wherever you can.

Most of my mates let the hormones take over and ended up at the social with squalling kids, nowhere to live and a boyfriend who had done a runner as soon as he found out she was pregnant.

The boys just wanted the fun but not the responsibility. At least I learnt from their mistakes.

By the time I was 14 I was at the local family planning clinic and insisting I be put on the pill. Mum had to give her consent as I was underage. Either she understood or just wasn't interested enough to care either way.

At least I could have some fun without the risks even if the boys did call me a slag.

Chapter 3:

Cecelia

Yah Hello. It's so sparkling that you want to talk to me.

Officially I'm Cecelia but my friends call me Sea, well actually, Lady C.

Does this mean I will be on the front cover of Hello magazine alongside the Wags?

That bitch Tara will be soo jealous.

About me, well we live in Hampshire. I can't believe that some of the poorer people call it a mansion. We do have a lot of acreage, but I only have one pony. Imagine!

There are just a few servants; a housekeeper, a cook and one gardener plus his helper, who I think is mentally retarded, a few girls to clean, and the chauffeur for Daddy.

Not a lot when you think about it.

Daddy works in the city so he usually has to stay in town during the week. We only really see him at weekends. Even then he often has to entertain clients at home, but usually they are old and boring, so unless he insists on me attending a function I try to escape.

The available males are few and far between. The only options are sons of Daddy's colleagues who tend to be nerds or do as some of my friends do, go for a bit of rough.

Can you blame me for escaping to the West End night-clubs whenever I can to try to get a bit of life?

I know Daddy loves me to bits even though they told me from an early age that I was adopted. Apparently Mummy has some problem where she can't produce and Daddy needed a son and heir. After adopting my brother Mummy insisted on having a girl to complete the family.

So here I am.

Sometimes I do wonder about my natural parents, but on the whole I have a good life, so why rock the boat?

What horror if I tracked them down and found they were low class plebs living on a council estate. Best not to look any further.

As it is, my friends include minor royalty and I get invites to all the major social events even if I am only on the B-list.

I like my life even if it is a bit boring sometimes.

I can't wait to get to uni and really start having some fun.

Chapter 4:

Delphine

I was christened Delphine.

My mother was French and wanted to be a famous actress and singer.

She moved to London to further her career. Although she was young and pretty she never got the fame she craved.

After her latest boyfriend deserted her she took a job as a maid in a big house to make ends meet.

Although not the best person in the world at keeping a house clean, she learnt a lot about how the upper crust lived. She discovered how they inveigled invitations to the most important social occasions and learnt to identify the best wines.

Her vibrant personality ensured she was a great favourite with the old soaks and titled gentlemen who were guests at the house. She understood how to keep them interested but at arm's length.

The small supply of expensive jewellery which she earned and treasured passed to me on her death. It became my salvation at the most difficult time in my life.

The youngest son of the household where she was working became besotted with her, and I believe she was genuinely fond of him.

Who knows how my life would have turned out if she hadn't found herself pregnant with me, and been thrown out by his family as unsuitable.

As I was growing up she often told me about her English 'MiLord' and hinted that I had blue blood in my veins.

Life was hard but happy until she met and married a man some years her senior when I was still in my teens.

At first he was delighted with his beautiful, vivacious young wife but gradually his true nature as a bully and a pervert emerged.

I was only fifteen when he tried to force himself into my bed one day when Mama was out. I knew he wouldn't stop so I packed my bags and left.

Mama cried and said she would leave him, but I knew by now she was under his control. He was rich and she would never be able to give up her comfortable life and start again with nothing.

I was on my own.

Chapter 5:

Eustace

I first saw Delphine working as a waitress in a rather seedy club a taxi driver took me to when I was away on business.

There was something about her that showed she was a cut above the rest, and she exuded natural class and poise.

She also had a pretty face and shapely figure. She wore the cheap, dowdy uniform with a style that made it look designer.

At first, when I offered her a job working for me, she showed that she was not as naive as she looked and declined. I always get what I want and eventually I managed to persuade her.

My first instincts had been correct.

She was pleasant and charming to my business colleagues and managed to flatter them but stay detached without causing any unpleasantness.

Even the other girls liked her and she had the unusual knack of being able to work with other women without causing jealousy.

A rare find.

To me her most admirable trait was that she knew when to keep her mouth shut.

I couldn't say the same for all my employees, male or female. There were occasions when some of the girls had to lose their pretty faces and a few of the men were caused to disappear.

On one occasion I saw that she had been cornered by a business rival who I distrusted. He had such a loyal entourage that I had never been able to bribe or persuade them to provide me with information about him.

Delphine was not to know the whole area was covered by closed circuit TV monitored 24/7 from a control centre.

In accordance with my standing instructions, security called me urgently to listen in and watch the scene before giving my ruling.

I must admit my feeling of relief as I followed the action. She was superb.

She gave nothing away and her agile mind anticipated every possible trap. If I hadn't known the truth, even I would have believed her.

So I let her keep her pretty face and I began to rely on her more and more as someone I could trust implicitly.

Chapter 6:

Frank

Unless you were very senior in the underworld or in the government department that officially doesn't exist, you will probably never have heard of Eustace.

He didn't appear on the 'Most Wanted' lists although he would have been right at the top.

His connections were at the very highest level both nationally and internationally, with several minor governments in his pocket.

So far, the most that we had been able to get him on had been a parking ticket, and a penalty of £100 for putting in his tax returns one day late.

Not surprisingly, both the chauffeur and the accountant were replaced within a week.

It had been my Father's life-long ambition to bring him to the full force of the law, but he died without ever finding the right witnesses or a suitable non-corruptible judge.

My father's choice of career was bizarre really when you know that my great, great grandfather was very high up in the Mafia. Perhaps it was not so strange, but more just a natural swing of the pendulum.

On the surface I was just an ordinary businessman. This supplied the necessary cover for me to travel extensively to various meetings abroad.

I was never officially on the government secret service books although I had the highest security clearance. Occasionally I was given a small business contract providing IT support, just to keep up my cover story.

Such is fate that my legitimate company gained a reputation as one of the best.

A senior, but as far as I knew straight member of Eustace's staff approached my organisation to review their networking and computer security arrangements.

It was an opportunity too good to miss so I made sure I attended the meeting personally.

That was where I met Delphine.

The nature of my work meant that I had never married or even come close to having a regular, steady girlfriend.

Although I loved women I had stayed detached, but for some reason she got under my skin.

Totally against my usual character I asked her out. Our first date turned into several until eventually we became lovers.

Chapter 7:

Growing closer

I knew from the start that Eustace was not a man to be crossed.

Even in the early days I noticed that if someone upset him they were suddenly not around anymore.

I hoped they had just been sacked, but in my heart I think I knew the truth.

Although he was always kind to me I realised that it was best to keep my smile wide, my legs crossed and my mouth shut, even if my ears were open.

It was after his arch rival had tried to corner me that I noticed the biggest change in Eustace's attitude towards me. It was almost as if he had seen and heard every word.

I felt as if I had been tested for a secret exam which I had managed to pass.

After that he talked a lot more openly when I was around, even when he was discussing business with his henchmen.

I noticed some startled glances from them at first, as if they thought he had forgotten I was there. When he just glared at them and carried on speaking they eventually relaxed, and just accepted my presence.

Apart from being pleasant to visitors I had never really had time for men friends.

Maybe Mum's boyfriends had had a greater effect on me than I thought.

So when I met Frank and he asked me out I couldn't understand why on earth I said yes.

I spent the next few evenings until our date thinking up excuses until eventually I decided I would just not turn up.

He hadn't given me his phone number, so I had no way of contacting him.

Then I persuaded myself that as he knew where I lived and worked I had better go. I only intended to say that I didn't want to see him again.

That didn't stop me spending hours deciding what to wear and reaching the designated restaurant twenty minutes early.

Thankfully he had arrived half an hour early, and was there to greet me.

He was the perfect gentleman. Although we both avoided discussing our home lives and jobs, we found plenty to talk about and the evening flew past.

When he dropped me home, with a smouldering look but only a quick chaste goodnight kiss, I readily agreed to meet him the following Sunday so we could spend the day together.

Chapter 8:
Hope for the future

I wasn't sure that Delphine would turn up for our date, but she was there early and we had a wonderful evening together.

She seemed to understand without explanations that I didn't want to talk too much about my personal life. Instead, we had heated debates about our favourite films and books. I found myself drawn to her more and more.

As well as being beautiful with a lovely personality, she was also clearly intelligent and was knowledgeable on a wide range of subjects.

Reading between the lines I got the impression she had not had a good education, but had learnt from life and experience.

When I took her home I had to use all my control not to take her to bed there and then. I didn't want to scare her off, so after arranging to see her again I left her with only a quick goodnight kiss.

She was ready and waiting when I turned up on the Sunday and she hurriedly got into the car, almost as if she didn't want to be seen.

We were a bit on edge at first, but I managed to take her hand when we went for a walk along the path by the river, and we both started to relax.

The sun was shining, the birds were singing, it was warm with a slight breeze blowing and she seemed to glory in the peace of the countryside.

On impulse I hired a rowing boat from the marina, and she even took the oars for a while when I stopped for a breather.

We moored at a waterfront pub for lunch and managed to get an outside table to watch the wildlife while we were eating.

She was enchanted by a family of ducks, with Mum encouraging all her brood in their first swimming lesson. I couldn't help laughing as her face changed from worried to a beaming smile when a particularly brave duckling tried to show off and got into difficulties.

Not to worry. Mum was there to give him a good scolding then guide him gently back to the others.

I didn't want the day to end, but I had a very early flight for a business trip the next day. Reluctantly I had to leave her, but I promised I would phone her from Dubai the following evening after she finished work.

Exceptionally I had even given her my mobile phone number, and told her to contact me at any time of the day or night if she needed me.

Chapter 9:

In for the long-term

I had never expected to fall in love, but after our wonderful day on the river I felt I had finally found my soul mate.

Frank was everything I could hope for and more.

Gentle, caring, strong, understanding, good-looking, serious and fun all rolled into one.

Then came the night he made love to me for the first time.

Although inexperienced I realised that he was not only very sexy, but also very generous in ensuring that I was totally satisfied before taking his own release.

Our relationship went from strength to strength, and I couldn't believe that he felt the same way about me as I did about him.

For a while life was perfect and I was happier than I had ever been.

The only fly in the ointment was Eustace, who seemed to be uneasy about my relationship, although he never said anything.

Maybe he had just got used to having me around or worried that I might resign to become a housewife and mother.

Even the thought of waking up every morning next to Frank made me tingle, although I knew we both still had certain secrets we hadn't told each other.

It was when he whisked me off for a romantic weekend in Paris that we first revealed more to each other about our lives and backgrounds.

He hinted about his father being more than a policeman, his ancestors being on the wrong side of the law, and that he had chosen to follow in his father's footsteps, rather than his Sicilian relatives.

Without giving anything away, I did indicate that I would be happier with an employer who was a little closer to the edge of respectability and fair play, and that the high turnover of staff was a little worrying.

Our conversation turned to happier topics and that was the night he asked me to marry him.

After celebrating with more than one bottle of champagne that was also the night we got carried away and forgot about precautions.

So it was that the triplets were conceived in the birthplace of their maternal grandmother.

Chapter 10: Joy and Fatherhood

I knew Dee had something on her mind.

She had been distracted all day, but when she kissed me goodbye at the airport she promised to tell me everything when I got back in a few days' time.

I phoned her every day I was away, but she only said it was something she needed to say face-to-face, not on the phone.

The trip dragged and I couldn't concentrate.

I had nightmares imagining her telling me she wanted out of our engagement and didn't want to see me anymore.

So you can imagine my relief when I rushed home from the airport to find her waiting at my flat, where she hesitantly admitted she was pregnant.

At first I picked her up and just swung her round and then I was worried that might not be good for the baby, so I put her down and told her to put her feet up.

I wanted to break out the champagne but then changed my mind and said a cup of tea might be better in her condition, then I kissed her again.

It was only then that the worried expression left her face and she teased me about being like a clucking hen.

She admitted she had been worried how I would take the news. She had been anxious I wouldn't be happy about such a commitment when we had only known each other such a short time.

As if I wouldn't be overjoyed that my beautiful Dee was going to give me a wonderful son or daughter!

That's when she admitted it might be more than one, probably twins but it could even be triplets.

Again her face relaxed when I told her, "Only three? I want a football team as soon as you're strong enough."

"Hold your horses, Mister," she laughed. "Let's get this instalment out of the way first."

When I took her to bed that evening I had to keep reminding myself not to get carried away and to take it gently.

Eventually she lost patience, and after telling me she wouldn't break and to make the most of it while I could, she took the initiative. That's when I discovered that beneath that cool exterior was the sexy, vibrant woman I had chosen.

Chapter 11:

Keeping quiet

Up until I found I was pregnant, I had carried on living in the apartment provided by Eustace in his main mansion.

It took a lot to get up the nerve to tell him that although I wanted to carry on working for him, I needed my own space and was moving out of the apartment.

He listened quietly for a while, and for some reason the hairs stood up on the back of my neck.

I began to wonder if I would be the next one to suddenly disappear without trace.

I think I would have preferred being shouted and yelled at, or told I was an ungrateful bitch after all he had done for me.

That would have been easier to cope with.

Instead, his steady gaze and sad smile gave me goose bumps. I felt really scared.

Finally he smiled and said, "You know I have always looked on you as the daughter I never had. You've been as loyal to me as any true child of mine could have ever been.

"I knew I could never compete with the young, good-looking man of your dreams but I tell you this, if ever he hurts you or lets you down just let 'Papa' know. I'll always be here for you if ever you are in trouble. Just call me.

"Meanwhile, I wish you every happiness. Now, let's drink a toast to what I hope is true and everlasting love."

I couldn't help myself.

Although I knew or guessed that he was not the most honourable man in the world he had shown me such kindness. I had to give him a big hug and a kiss on the cheek as I said "Thank you, Papa."

For a moment I thought I had gone too far as a strange look came over his face. It was almost as if he really was my father. He was showing all the emotions of losing a beloved daughter, while praying that the man she had chosen would make her happy.

For the first time I understood the meaning of 'Giving the bride away.'

I had always thought of it as a chauvinistic expression; now it seemed to take on a more loving connotation.

Despite the emotional moment, although I had more or less admitted that I was going to live with Frank, I had not mentioned my pregnancy.

One step at a time.

Chapter 12:

Living and learning

Dee moved in with me less than a week after telling me she was pregnant.

I had wanted to be with her when she told Eustace, but she had insisted on speaking to him herself.

Loving her as I did, even more so now she was carrying my offspring, I respected her right to do things her way but those were some of the worst days of my life.

She wouldn't even confirm on what particular time or day she was going to tell him she was moving out from living under his clutches, so I couldn't just 'happen' to be around.

All she would say was that the timing had to be right.

I didn't know whether to laugh at her insecurity, or cry with relief when she asked if I would be available to help her move the following Sunday, but only if it was convenient and if I still wanted all her clutter in my pristine flat.

As if it would worry me if she left the top off the toothpaste or we fought over the remote control, or argued over whether the toilet tissue should roll over or under.

That was just normal, loving life and I couldn't wait.

I was even looking forward to mopping her brow when she started suffering morning sickness and the hormones made her ratty and unreasonable.

My only concern now was how Eustace would take it when her pregnancy became obvious and she told him she was leaving the job.

I could only hope and pray that he truly looked on her as a daughter. Maybe he would accept her leaving his employment with the same grace he had accepted her moving out.

Knowing the man and his character through what my Father had told me of him when I was growing up, I still couldn't totally accept that he had given in so easily.

The best I could wish for was that with age he had mellowed, and had truly learnt a father's love for my Dee.

As the months passed we settled into living together as if it had been destined by the stars. Her belly started to swell and the signs of her pregnancy became obvious.

Normally it is the woman who starts arranging the venue, date, flowers and all the other paraphernalia of wedding arrangements while the groom sits back and says 'Yeah, just tell me when and where.'

In our case it was the other way round. I was hinting about setting the date, she was the one saying there was plenty of time.

Chapter 13:
Murder

Hand on heart, those were some of the happiest days of my life.

Even when the sickness and the insecurities set in, and she couldn't believe she was still the most beautiful and desirable woman in the world, my life was perfect.

It was my job to make her smile again and prove how much I loved her.

Whether her breasts were hand-size and pert or overflowing, whether her belly was flat or providing a safe haven for my children she was always my dream woman.

I hated having to leave her even for a day, but I had to make sure my normal business made a profit to provide for my future family.

I had gradually decreased my involvement in my alternative occupation and had seriously thought of withdrawing altogether, so I could concentrate on living a normal life.

Maybe my father would understand that Eustace had been his war not mine. I had found something more important to concentrate on.

All that changed when a contact sent me a message through an established covert network that there was trouble afoot.

One of the undercover agents who had been on the Eustace investigation had been found dead in suspicious circumstances.

I had worked with the guy before on various secret projects.

He was a hard working family man, straight as a die and I felt sick to my stomach.

Maybe it was nothing to do with Eustace, but my love and my unborn children were at risk.

Now it was personal.

I had to get involved and find out the truth whatever the cost.

All that was important was Dee and the babies. Even if I wasn't around to see them grow, I would always know that my blood and my genes were carrying on.

Life went on. The fact that Dee was carrying triplets was confirmed, although the odds for this happening naturally were four thousand to one.

Not a day passed when I didn't worry about her; not just the normal worries of pregnancy, but whether we would ever be able to have a traditional peaceful life without unsavoury outside influences.

Chapter 14:
No place to hide

I wanted to cancel my business appointment when Dee's time came close, but she insisted she would be fine.

She wanted me to go on this trip before the triplets were born. She joked that once they arrived I would have my every waking moment taken up with changing nappies and feeding them, while she slept and made the most of being cosseted.

Reluctantly I agreed although I had a bad feeling.

I put it down to the nervousness of being a father for the first time and tried to concentrate on tying up loose ends in the business, so I could take time off with a clear conscience.

The first night I was away she sounded happy and relaxed when I phoned her, and I managed to calm down slightly. The next evening she sounded a little unsure, and I started to worry again. The third evening there was no answer and I panicked.

I carried on phoning every hour, on the hour, until at three o'clock in the morning, London time, a sleepy voice answered and berated me for waking her at such an ungodly hour.

I have never been so relieved in all my life.

It seems she thought she had started labour and had taken herself off to hospital just to be told it was a false alarm. Once she got home she had intended to phone me but had fallen asleep.

Despite her traumatic day, she ended up apologising for causing me to worry. She told me how much she loved me and to hurry home as soon as I could.

The journey from the airport seemed endless. When I finally got to the flat I slammed the doors open shouting her name, my mind working overtime at what I would find.

Although it was only three o'clock in the afternoon, I didn't realise how much I had been holding my breath until a sleepy voice called from the bedroom, "Can you keep the noise down? An expectant mother is trying to get some rest in here."

I hugged her as if I would never let her out of my sight again until eventually my heartbeat slowed and I could breathe again.

It was only when she was wrapped in my arms in the early hours of the following morning, after I had cooked a meal which she devoured but I hardly touched, that she quietly asked what was worrying me.

She knew I had more on my mind than just the normal worries of an expectant father, and bit-by-bit, I told her some of my concerns.

Chapter 15:

Only time will tell

I knew Frank was looking forward to being a father and was naturally nervous, but I could sense there was something else worrying him.

As this was my first pregnancy I had expected to be insecure, but having been on my own for most of my life, I was surprised how much I had grown to depend on his presence and support.

I felt ashamed of myself for panicking when I thought my contractions had started. I was even more embarrassed when the experienced midwives almost patted me on the head as if I was a silly child and sent me home again.

I wanted Frank around to reassure me, but at the same time didn't want to face him and let him know how stupid I had been.

Several times I picked up the phone, but eventually I dozed off without completing the call.

It was only when I heard his voice that I began to appreciate how selfish I had been in not letting him know everything was fine. I had just become unstrung and needy.

How on earth had I managed to find such a wonderful man to love me?

Not once did he give me the ticking off I deserved.

Instead he was just loving and caring, as if it was his fault he wasn't there when I needed him.

It was only when we were cuddled up in bed after he had cooked me a lovely meal, with one eye on the pots and the other constantly watching me, that he gave any indication of what was on his mind.

I knew that he had always distrusted Eustace, but I had just put it down to his father's influence.

That night he opened up more than he ever had before. Unwittingly he validated my secret fears and confirmed the intuitions that I had tried to put down to my over active hormones.

We even discussed the almost surreal scenario of what we would do if the worst happened. How would we communicate if, for some reason, we were left wondering about the others unexpected disappearance?

Almost jokingly we agreed that however many years had passed, we would meet on the bridge over the river Seine at nine p.m. local time, on the twenty-ninth of September.

Although at the time it felt silly, I knew in my heart that it was an assignation neither of us would ever forget. We could laugh at it together when we were in our dotage.

Chapter 16:

Pregnancy

The next morning I woke in a panic, but as my eyes flew open I found my beloved Dee snoring gently in my arms. She must have felt me stir as she quietly woke and gave me her angelic smile.

"Hi you," she said, "Nice to have you around again."

I felt as if my heart would burst. If this was what love was I never wanted to be without it. As I went to kiss her she returned my greeting with passion, but then with a wry smile said, "Sorry, Hon. The joys of pregnancy. I need the bathroom, like now!"

How could you not adore this woman who could be nearly nine months pregnant and still be the sexiest, most innocent woman on this earth.

As she was so close to bringing my children into the world I couldn't show my love in a physical way. It was still the happiest time of my life so far and we had all our future before us.

I held her close, kissed her like I would never let her go and worked hard to stop my heart bursting with the joy of finally finding such love.

Although her projected confinement date was so near, she refused to let me stay home the next day and insisted I took the quick business trip to Paris. She was laughing as she told me I could probably get home quicker from there than I could from another appointment in the North of England.

The next morning I kissed her goodbye and said I would be home before she even got out of bed.

That was the last time I saw her.

When I dashed home from the airport the following day after a frustrating delay caused by air traffic controller strikes, an instinct told me before I even opened the door that the flat was empty.

Nevertheless, I rushed around calling her name and searching every room.

I tried to convince myself that it was just the babies making their appearance, and prayed I would be in time to see them come into the world.

Getting no reply I rushed to the private hospital to be met with a wall of silence and uncomfortable non-answers.

Everyone I spoke to just referred me up to a higher level, putting obstacles in my way at every turn, making every excuse that I was not registered as her husband or legal partner, nothing but bullshit.

What was going on? Where was she? What had happened? Where was the love of my life and my offspring? Were they OK?

Chapter 17:
Quitting life

Eventually, just before I totally lost it and had the indignity of being thrown out by security, a very senior doctor spoke to me. He told me that Dee had checked into the hospital in the very early hours of this morning.

He informed me that she had delivered a stillborn child and been collected by her father, who had taken her home to comfort her in her loss.

I went totally demented, screaming at the doctor she was having triplets not one baby, she had never known her father. How could they let this happen? She had been kidnapped. I was going to the police. What had happened to my children?

Finally I burst into tears of frustration, and was almost forcibly ejected and put in a taxi home.

Although both of my jobs, the legal and the clandestine one had meant I needed to keep a cool detached head, I lost control and stopped thinking rationally.

I intended rushing round to Eustace's mansion, taking on all the security guards single-handedly and threatening or torturing him until he revealed what he had done with Dee.

The only thing that stopped me was the sudden appearance of three very large and tooled up guys who I knew worked for my secret employers.

These were no dumbo brawn and no brain tough guys, but highly intelligent and trusted members of the organisation.

I suppose I should have been flattered that the powers that be had sent three of them. Even so, it took a hypodermic needle to subdue me enough for them to take me to the highest security level meeting I had ever been obliged to attend.

When I came round, it was to find myself sitting in a chair in front of the number one man, who few people even knew existed.

He started off by apologising for the heavy-handed treatment. Obviously intelligence had made him well aware of all the circumstances surrounding my involvement with Eustace and Dee.

For a man in his position, he showed unusual compassion and understanding of my concern for Dee and the babies. Despite that, he made it clear that whatever had happened to them would not be enough to jeopardise the current investigation.

Until a conclusion was reached one way or another, I was to be taken secretly out of the country to an unknown destination, with no access to my passport or means of returning to the UK.

The staff at my office had already been told that I was taking time off as my partner had suffered a miscarriage, and for the time being I would be out of touch.

Chapter 18:

Reunion

When the pains started I tried at first to ignore them, kidding myself it was just another false alarm, but this time I knew it was the real thing.

My first thought was to phone Frank, but just as I picked up my mobile the door opened and Eustace walked in accompanied by two paramedics.

He told me everything was under control and not to worry. Frank had been informed and would meet me at the hospital. I was just to relax, everything would be fine.

After that it was a blank.

I woke up in a luxurious room with nurses dancing attendance on me. From the smell I guessed it was a private clinic.

“Where’s Frank?” was my first comment.

"You were out for the count," I was told. "He has been here for days, but left an hour ago for a business meeting."

Then everything went blank again.

In a haze I was half aware of the sound of several voices, one of which I identified as belonging to Eustace, together with others who I assumed were doctors.

When I finally came round and started to feel more human, I tricked a junior nurse into unwittingly putting me in the picture.

When I said I needed something to do she brought me that evening's newspaper to read. After browsing the headlines I glanced at the date. After checking several times and forcing my brain to focus I realised that well over a week had passed since I had felt the contractions.

Before I had time to concentrate my scrambled brain, Eustace appeared in the doorway with an enormous bunch of flowers. He sat on the bed, stroked my hand, and told me how sorry he was about my miscarriage.

It was as if he was truly my father. He sounded so concerned and upset for me, reassuring me that it often happened with first pregnancies, and that as I was so strong and healthy it wouldn't be long before I was holding a new baby in my arms.

That made me ask about Frank again.

He seemed reluctant to talk about him, only saying I had enough to worry about at the moment and there were plenty more fish in the sea for a young, beautiful woman like me.

Finally he told me he had been arrested and deported to Sicily for crimes against humanity.

Chapter 19:

Secrets

At first I refused to believe the evidence of my own eyes, but eventually with no sign of Frank I had to accept what I had been told as the truth.

It was only then I began to register that on the night I was due to give birth the front door was locked and only Frank and I had keys.

How had Eustace managed to get in with the paramedics? I switched between not trusting Eustace and believing that I should have known Frank was too good to be true.

My now flat belly proved that I was no longer pregnant and I mourned my lost babies.

As I regained my strength I questioned Eustace about them. He told me that for a while my life hung in the balance and it wasn't thought that I would survive.

He had arranged a quiet but dignified ceremony for my three lost souls. He promised that when I was stronger he would take me to the crematorium to see the memorial plaques he had organised.

I remembered joking with Frank about needing names for the babies, who we had laughingly referred to as A, B, and C.

Although I never remember telling Eustace about it, he eventually admitted that he had had them christened although they were stillborn. He had given them the names Abigail, Beatrice and Cecelia.

I didn't know whether to love him for his thoughtfulness or distrust him for finding out something that I believed was a secret.

Time passed. Gradually I regained my strength, and although I never forgot Frank or the triplets I learnt to live again.

I still had nightmares, but sometimes wonderful dreams where I was living in a beautiful home with three adorable toddlers. I was laughing with them as Frank came home from work and joined me on the floor to play with our children before we put them to bed.

When I awoke from these dreams it always took me a while to get back to reality.

Years passed.

I started working for Eustace again, but whatever I was doing I always made a point of being alone on the evening of the 29th September. I would drink a lonely bottle of wine and raise a silent toast to what might have been.

Eustace was now an old man. When he died that August, I was astounded to learn from his lawyers that he had left me enough money to be comfortable for the rest of my life.

Chapter 20:
Trio

Although I had grown more and more to think of Delphine as the daughter I never had, I also knew that as long as Frank was around following in his father's footsteps, I would never have peace.

It was a disaster when she became pregnant by him.

This was something I needed to control. There was always the possibility that the truth would come out and they would grow up to continue the vendetta against me.

Although I considered the possibility, I could not bring myself to authorise the normal procedure for when someone was causing me problems.

Like a stupid, senile, weak old man I had even started to look on the triplets as my grandchildren. Eventually I compromised.

It would be announced that they were born dead and suitable funeral arrangements would be made. Meanwhile, my money and influence would ensure that they were shipped out to families independently, as if each was the sole birth child of a young unmarried mother.

The sad story would be told of the young girl of dubious morals, whose only wish was to get shot of the unwanted daughter as soon as possible, so she could revert to her unfettered, carefree life.

It was given out that she had no interest whatsoever in knowing or hearing about the unwelcome interruption to her previously unencumbered life.

Anyone looking to adopt the child was given no indication that she was actually one of triplets. The adoptive parents were made to sign a legal document that in no circumstances would they ever attempt to trace the true parentage.

Even I was not made aware of the names of the families who were adopting the girls.

Through a long and tangled network the appropriate arrangements were made. Each child was deliberately placed in a different class of family so the chances of them meeting up accidentally, or being sent to the same school were reduced to minimal odds.

I made sure Delphine had the best treatment money could buy. Gradually she reverted to more or less her old self although I sometimes caught her with a faraway look in her eyes.

When I asked her what she was thinking, she always smiled and said, "Nothing special." She never regained the original spark and love of life that she had when I first met her.

I put it down to age creeping up as it does on all of us.

Chapter 21:

United

Daddy had insisted that I be there as hostess for his summer ball.

Mummy wasn't feeling well. Now that I was an adult, he thought it would be good experience for me to take on all the arrangements.

Actually, it was quite fun liaising with the various party planners and designers to ensure the party was superb enough to make the gossip pages.

I had never realised just how much was involved. I had to call on all my contacts and put the erudition from my University degree into practice.

Still, I was bright and a quick learner. I finally understood the importance of not just sending out invitations to the right people, but making sure there was someone to arrange the flowers and wash up after the sumptuous menu was served.

Although I never met the party planner until the actual evening of the ball, I was surprised how easily we communicated by e-mail leading up to the event.

It was as if she could read my mind and anticipate what I wanted before I could put it into words.

I don't know why Mummy always got so stressed. This was fun and everything was going swimmingly. All it needed was someone to show who was in charge to get things done.

Everything went off perfectly, and when the final guest left Daddy was over the moon.

I was happy knowing that we would definitely make the pages of the best society magazines.

My training had taught me that it was good form to thank everyone who had assisted in the success, so I sought out Abigail, the party planner whose designs had been such a talking point.

I was told she was in the kitchen enjoying some late refreshments now that her duties had been completed.

Although Mummy regularly looked in on the kitchen staff, I didn't often descend down there so it felt strangely unfamiliar territory.

Even that didn't explain the surreal experience when I pushed open the door to find myself almost in a hall of mirrors.

Even though the two girls in deep conversation at the table wore different clothes, had different hairstyles, and were obviously from different backgrounds, they looked identical.

What was even more astounding was that they looked exactly like me!

Chapter 22: Validation

Despite my exclusive finishing school my mouth dropped open and I just gaped.

At least the other two were doing the same as we all three stared at each other in amazement.

It was Abigail who broke the atmosphere by explaining she had popped down to the kitchen to thank the staff for their help. She had come across Bea washing up and realised they could be twins.

It seemed such an unbelievable coincidence they had sat down together and started discussing their backgrounds and upbringing.

To their astonishment they discovered they were the same age, born on the same day, the 29th September, and both had been adopted.

Abigail had once tried to trace her natural parents but had always hit brick walls so had eventually given up.

I finally managed to find my voice even if it only came out as an unflattering squeak.

“That’s my birthday too,” I whispered, “And I was adopted as well.”

We all sat together at the servant’s table and talked non-stop until the early hours of the morning.

Despite our different accents and upbringings it was surprising how much we had in common. We instinctively seemed to anticipate what the others were thinking and feeling.

It was eerie but also in some ways comforting. We were even in agreement that we had all in some way felt as if a part of us was missing.

Without even discussing it we knew that we would stay in touch and meet up regularly.

I didn’t sleep at all that night, and Daddy noticed how tired I looked when I went down to breakfast the following morning.

He put it down to the excitement of the ball and congratulated me on doing a superb job.

I explained what had happened. After listening carefully he said he wanted to meet the others to see for himself.

After that, he gave us his wholehearted support in tracking down our natural parents. With his money, influence, and contacts, we were able to make much better headway than Abigail had on her own.

Chapter 23:

When and where

In the weeks after the death of Eustace, I was kept busy with making funeral arrangements and handling the various problems that arose when he was no longer there to control things.

His large staff and business associates seemed to turn naturally to me as his confidante, although it was the lawyers who were theoretically in control of the administration of his estate.

Nevertheless, I found myself called upon to use all my skills and discretion in fielding nonstop telephone calls and visits when the lawyers remained incommunicado, and didn't respond to urgent demands.

Perhaps because I had been at Eustace's side for so long, and was someone they knew and trusted, I was looked upon as his natural successor even though I had no legal authority.

Eventually I managed to get things running as smoothly as was possible under the circumstances, but felt exhausted after the nonstop hassles of the last few weeks.

Glancing at the calendar I realised we were already well into September.

It suddenly hit me that I was a rich woman. Before I could give it conscious thought I had booked a short first class trip to Paris to take a break.

Sitting alone at dinner in my five-star hotel, on the evening of the 28th September, I began to wonder what on earth had possessed me to book this lonely trip.

Maybe I just needed to escape from the hustle and issues following Eustace's death. Subconsciously a part of me had never forgotten Frank, particularly on our special day.

I had often wondered whether it was fate intervening that had made us choose that date, which had turned out to be the same day I miscarried our triplets.

Although over the years I had grown a thick skin and become self-sufficient, underneath the hard exterior still beat the heart of the young, naïve girl who had fallen passionately and permanently in love with a man who in the end had deserted her without a second thought.

That didn't stop me being on the Pont des Arts in the evening of the 29th September, after eating an early meal at the hotel.

I soaked up the atmosphere, watched the world go by and people watched, along with all the other tourists and native Parisians.

It made me think of my mother and remember her vivacity when I was just a young girl. Obviously my thoughts also turned to my own children who I had never seen, and the man whose seed had given them life.

Chapter 24: Xplanations

With tears blurring my eyes, I did a double take at the tall, mature but still good-looking man standing with what were obviously his three daughters, watching the waters of the Seine flowing below.

As I turned away, ashamed of showing so much emotion in a public place something about him made me look back and our eyes met.

"Dee," I heard him call and then louder, "Dee. It is you. Dee, wait!" before he was rushing towards me and I was enveloped in the same bear hug I remembered from when I first told him I was pregnant.

"Frank? It can't be! I don't believe it," I managed to splutter before I dissolved into tears that would not stop flowing.

Unnoticed, the three girls who I could now see were identical came up to stand and stare at us.

Trying to stem my tears I finally managed to turn to them, waiting for Frank to introduce me to his daughters from the unknown woman he had obviously met and married.

His actual words took my breath away. "Meet your mother," was what he said.

"Dee, meet A, B, and C, our daughters."

It was all too much.

I had come to Paris berating myself for being the stupidest of daydreaming romantics. Now it felt so surreal I was sure I would wake up soon to find myself back in the reality of my normal everyday life.

It took a long while, and a lot of tears, and talking and interruptions, and interrogations, and kisses and more tears before an outline of what had occurred actually began to sink into my befuddled brain.

I spent the night with Frank in his hotel bed with the girls sleeping in the suite next door.

When he made love to me it was as if we had never been apart, and the years slipped away.

It was only when I was cuddled up safely in his arms that he was able to properly explain how he was, to all intents and purposes, kidnapped and forcibly stopped from contacting me.

The miscarriage had never happened. The girls were born healthy and farmed out to adoptive parents as a further ploy to keep us apart.

Chapter 25:

Y?

"Why did things go so wrong?" I asked Frank.

"We met; I fell in love with you. You were everything to me.

"I was scared when I got pregnant, but your reaction was everything I could have wished for. You made me feel beautiful even when I got fat and had morning sickness.

"For the first time in my life I was with someone I trusted one hundred percent and you were there with me all the way. I couldn't have asked for anything more.

"Then, when I needed you more than I have ever needed anything in my life you disappeared.

"I had to face the blackness and the birth and thinking I had lost the babies alone. You were nowhere around.

“The only one there to take care of me was Eustace. Even if I had always felt I could never trust him he was the one who helped to get me through things in the blackest days of my life.”

After probably the longest, most heartfelt speech of her life, Delphine finally stopped letting out all the emotions of the previous twenty odd years.

Lifting her eyes to look at Frank she was amazed to see he had tears in his eyes.

“My darling. How can you ever forgive me?

“I know before I met you my father’s influence overshadowed my life, but I wanted to give it all up so we could have a normal life together.

“I was ready to cut off all ties with the government and even tolerate Eustace but they wouldn’t let me go.

“There was too much at stake and I knew too much. They wouldn’t let me go.

“They knew how much I would give up for you, that you were the most important thing in my life.

“They made sure I had no way of contacting you. I was kept a prisoner so I could never let you know what had actually happened to stop me being with you.

“I never forgot you and every day I berated myself for letting you down. I dreamt of you every night, but never thought fate would ever give me the opportunity to see you again.

“I will willingly spend the rest of my life trying to put things right if you let me.”

Chapter 26:

Zenith

That night I slept better than I had for twenty years.

Coming round slowly from my beautiful dream, I stretched and was reluctant to wake up. I just wanted to sink back into sleep so I could relive every wonderful moment before facing the world alone again.

I felt I was still dreaming when Frank's face appeared and with a huge smile on his face called, "Wake up sleepyhead. Breakfast is ready and we've still got a lot of catching up to do.

"The girls have been up for hours and can't wait to see their Mum again to talk about all the missing years.

"Four women. God, what have I done to deserve this?

"One poor man doesn't stand a chance, but I wouldn't change it for the world."

As I took a quick shower and hurriedly dressed, my heart was light as I jokingly fought off my wonderful man who wanted to take me back to bed. I had to remind him our daughters were waiting for us.

After all, we now had all the time in the world to be a proper family.

What lessons would I pass on to my daughters?

Trust your instincts. Never give up. Believe in kismet.

Keep your promises, however long it takes.

Dreams do come true. Believe me, I and my family are the living proof.